MW00892379

Big
Red
Balloon

BENJAMIN MONKEY
NO BITING!

Little Benjamin was a fun little monkey.

He liked to play every day with friends.

But he had real trouble with his mouth.

One day his friend Panda came to play ball.

"I go first," said Panda. But Benjamin wanted the ball.

Benjamin tried to bite Panda on the arm. "No!" said Panda.

Panda went home mad.

"Benjamin Monkey, no biting. Biting hurts!" said his mom.

The next day Benjamin's friend Giraffe came to visit.

Giraffe was eating candy. It looked good to eat.

But Benjamin had no candy.

This made Benjamin sad.

He tried to bite Giraffe on his hand.

"No Benjamin!" said Giraffe and he ran back home.

"Benjamin Monkey, no biting. Biting hurts!" said his father.

One day Benjamin saw his friend Rabbit with a kite. "Come fly my kite," said Rabbit. Benjamin liked flying the kite.

"My turn," said Rabbit.

But Benjamin did not want to stop.

Rabbit tried to take the kite back. But Benjamin tried to bite Rabbit.

"No!" said Rabbit and he ran home with his kite.

"Benjamin Monkey, no biting. Biting hurts!" said his mother.

One day Benjamin saw all his friends playing games at the park.

Benjamin wanted to play too.

But Rhino said, "Benjamin you can not play with us."

"Why not?" asked Benjamin.

"Benjamin you bite when you play," said Rhino.

This made Benjamin very mad.

"I want to play!" said Benjamin.

This time Benjamin did bite his friend.

"Ouch!" yelled Rhino. Rhino ran home crying.

Benjamin walked home very sad.

No friends would play with him.

At home his mom asked, "Did you bite your friend Rhino?"

"Yes," said Benjamin sadly.

"You may not bite people," said his dad. "Biting hurts!"

"We must go to see if Rhino is hurt," said his mom.

So Benjamin left to visit Rhino.

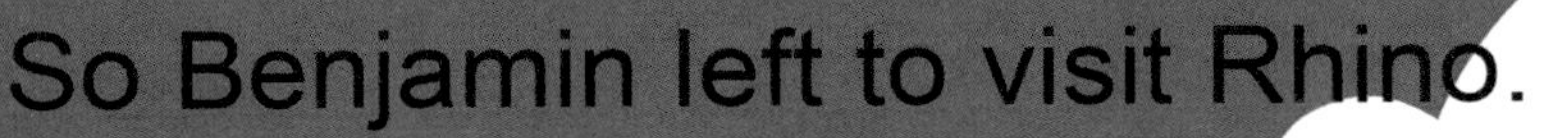

"Does your arm hurt?" asked Benjamin's mom.

"Yes," cried Rhino. Benjamin felt very sad.

He did not mean to hurt his friend.

Rhino's mom and dad hugged little Rhino.

Benjamin's mom asked, "How can we make Rhino feel better?"

Benjamin said, "I know!"

Benjamin ran to Rhino's room to get Rhino's favorite toy.

Benjamin said, "I'm sorry for biting you Rhino."

Rhino stopped crying.

At home Benjamin's mom said, "Benjamin you must use words. Never bite. Biting hurts."

"You must try to use words to say how you feel," said his mom.

"Okay I will try," said Benjamin.

"Say, please share the ball Panda," said his mom.

"Say, may I please have some candy Giraffe."

"Say, may I please fly the kite Rabbit."
"Do you see?" asked his mom.

"Yes I do. Use words but never bite,"
said Benjamin.

The next day Benjamin went to Rhino's house.

Rhino had a new bike.

"Do you like my new bike?" asked Rhino.

"Yes," said Benjamin. Benjamin wanted to ride the bike.

But Rhino did not get off the bike.

Benjamin grabbed Rhino's arm.

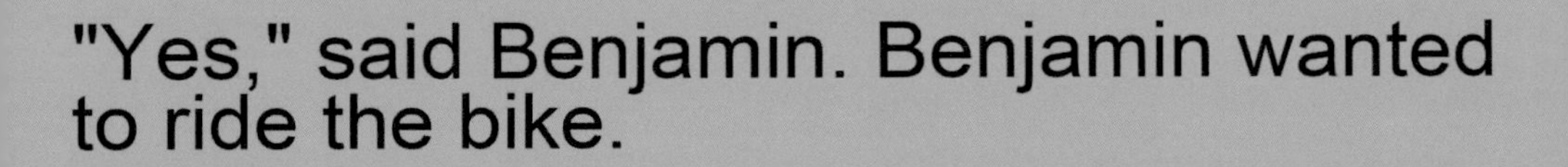

But Benjamin wanted to do as his mom had said.

Never bite. Use words.

So Benjamin said, "Rhino can I please ride your bike?"

"Yes you can ride my bike," said Rhino.

Benjamin was very happy.

Benjamin did not bite his friends ever again.

He used words.

Made in the USA
Lexington, KY
29 January 2019